His Majesty the DEMON KING'S Housekeeper

This is the Demon King's initial design. Why is he prettier here than he is now?!

Of all things she could be the saint of, it's cleaning. A little on the short side, but she's moderately endowed.
The pint-sized heroine. High schooler.
Familiar: the heroine's navigator. She can transform into a cute girl.
I gave her a bob cut since so many of the men in this story have long hair. In black-and-white pages, her hair is black, but I'll give it a touch of color for the color pages.
I want to keep her in her school uniform as much as possible to make it obvious that the heroine is from Japan (another world) while she's in the demon realm.
This is Sakura's preliminary design!
SHE HAD BLACK HAIR!
She gets transported to another world on the way home from working with the beautification committee over summer break.

His Majesty the DEMON KING'S Housekeeper

OUR DIFFEREN-CES ARE ONE REASON WE ARE SO PRO-TECTIVE OF OUR SPIRITUAL CULTURE AND SYMBOLS.
FESTIVALS BEING ONE...
AND HOLDING COURT WITH HIS UNIVER-SALLY ADORED MAJESTY FOR ANOTHER.
BUT IF THE UNCLEAN ASH CONTINUES TO FALL...
EVEN THOSE MAY BE TAKEN FROM US.
TOUCH
SO, WHILE I KNOW HOW EAGER YOU ARE TO RETURN TO YOUR OWN WORLD...
GLOW
SAKURA...
I'M EVER SO GLAD THAT YOU CAME TO OURS.
FLICK
FLICK
AH-HA!
DID THAT PLEASE YOU?
IT DID, DIDN'T IT?

Afterword: Several days later...
LOOK, SAKURA! THEY WROTE ABOUT YOUR EXPLOITS AT THE TOMATO FESTIVAL IN THIS COPY OF *THE DEGENERATE*!
AREN'T YOU EX-CITED?
IT'S PRETTY COOL, BUT I JUST DID SOME LAUNDRY.
YOU'RE ALWAYS SO HAPPY WHILE YOU'RE CLEANING, BUT YOU NEVER SEEM TO CARE ABOUT YOUR GROWTH IN POPULARITY.
OF COURSE NOT! I JUST DID WHAT CAME NATURALLY!
SERI-OUSLY, MILIA.
WHY WOULD THEY HOLD A FESTIVAL WHEN THE WITCH'S CURSE IS STILL CAUSING THE ASH TO FALL?
WE DON'T *FORGET* ABOUT IT, IF THAT'S WHAT YOU'RE ASKING. WE SIMPLY DON'T WANT TO GIVE UP ON OUR TRADI-TIONS.
SURELY YOU'VE NOTICED THAT NO TWO DEMON BEASTS ARE ALIKE, YES?

Afterword

Hello. I'm Saiko Wadori, the writer behind *His Majesty the Demon King's Housekeeper.*

If I'm being honest, light novels are my usual area of expertise. I specialize in kicking good-looking men down the slope of misfortune, and it was that style of mine that connected me to Mika Kajiyama-sensei and the Princess editorial department as a candidate for co-author. The summoning spell they used was something along the lines of, "Do you want to write a frenetic shojo rom-com about a heroine who was summoned from another world and her misfortunate sexy paramour?"

Now, that was right up my alley!

After that critical hit landed, this is what I came up with. I hope you've enjoyed it so far.

I've worked with Kajiyama-sensei previously on one of my older titles, *Koushu-sama no Oyakusoku!,* when she drew the insert pages for a series about a misfortunate emperor. This time she's taking her pen to a story about a misfortunate demon king. She's on her way to drawing a complete series of *misfortunate majesties.* ☆

(Who's making her do this, again? Oh, right. Me.)

But I digress. I will say that, as a huge shojo manga buff, I've purchased Princess comics ever since I was a teenager and I'm very familiar with the brand. Publishing my own creation under their label is like a dream come true. I hope you continue to enjoy the series! (Bow)

Saiko Wadori

His Majesty the DEMON KING'S Housekeeper

His Majesty the DEMON KING'S Housekeeper

SAINT SAKU-RA...?
Chapter 4/End
His Majesty the Demon King's Housekeeper
Volume 1/End

PUBLIC OPINION OF SAINT SAKURA HAS RISEN ONCE AGAIN.
MM-HM.
AND YOU MUST BE THRILLED THAT YOUR SAINT-STAMPED PRODUCT LINE IS TAKING OFF, LEHAYE.
I SUPPOSE I AM.
IT IS A GOOD THING THAT WORD OF THE SAINT'S MIRACLES HAS SPREAD, YOUR MAJESTY.
IT HAS DONE WONDERS TO CONSOLIDATE YOUR RULE THROUGHOUT THE REALM.
AND YET...IF WORD OF HER MIRACLES SPREADS *TOO* FAR...
IT MAY VERY WELL INVITE DISASTER.

OKAY!
THROB
HMM...? NOW, WAS THAT MY IMAGINATION, OR DID MY EARS BEHOLD THE BITTERSWEET PLUCKING OF HEART-STRINGS?
IT CAN ONLY MEAN ONE THING... IT'S AWAKEN-ED.
WHAT HAS?
HIS MAJESTY THE DEMON KING'S PURE HEART.

AND SO, A QUICK TRIP TO CHECK OUT THE FESTIVAL TURNED INTO A SLEEPOVER.
THE SAINT REALLY CAN MAKE MIRACLES!
IT WASN'T A MIRACLE. WHEN TOMATO PIGMENTS ARE EXPOSED TO ULTRAVIOLET RAYS, THEY NATURALLY DISAPPEAR.
ANYONE CAN GET THEM OUT, AS LONG AS YOU KNOW HOW!
I WAS A LITTLE SCARED AT FIRST...
BUT I'M GLAD THAT SCIENCE IS NO DIFFER-ENT HERE THAN IN MY WORLD!
HEH...
TOMATO STAINS WILL DISAPPEAR WHEN THEY COME IN CONTACT WITH UV RAYS, BUT THAT DOESN'T MEAN THE GUNK WILL GO AWAY. SO BE SURE TO WASH THEM OUT FIRST, THEN HANG THEM OUT TO DRY!
IF YOU GET RID OF THE COLOR WITHOUT THE GUNK, THEN IT'LL START TO STINK AND ATTRACT BUGS.
SAKURA. COME.
THE PALACE AWAITS.

HUH? DID I JUST HEAR SOME-THING?
IN YOUR IMAGI-NATION.
THE STAINS ARE ALL GONE!
BUT YESTER-DAY THEY WOULDN'T COME OUT AT ALL!

THEN...
I'LL BE SAFE FROM GHOSTS AS LONG AS I'M WITH YOU, RIGHT?
THROB

I DON'T UNDER-STAND YOU.
WHEN YOU WERE SURROUNDED BY HAIRY DEMON BEASTS, YOU DIDN'T EVEN FLINCH.
'CAUSE ...
I CAN SEE DEMON BEASTS...
B-BUT I CAN'T STAND SPIRITUAL THINGS LIKE GHOSTS AND EVIL SPIRITS THAT'RE INVISIBLE.
THEY AREN'T COMMON-PLACE HERE, ARE THEY...?
EVEN IF THEY WERE, THEY WOULDN'T DARE SHOW THEMSELVES TO THE DEMON KING.

FWOOSH
IT'S ALREADY DARK OUTSIDE...
ZWOOP
BOING
GH-GHOST ?!
WHAT IS IT?
A GHOST!
THERE'S A GH-GHOST OUTSIDE THE WIN-DOW!
KREE
OH.
CAN YOU STAND?
YES...

I COULDN'T EVEN IF I TRIED, MAJESTY. THERE IS NO ROOM FOR ANYTHING IN HER MIND BUT LAUNDRY.
BUT IF I MAY BE SO BOLD, MAJESTY, YOU COULD ALWAYS TRY PULLING HER AWAY YOURSELF.
......

I'M DOING EVERY-THING RIGHT, BUT THE STAIN WON'T COME OUT.
NO WORRIES. THE NUM-BERS ARE ON OUR SIDE!
EVERY-ONE, JUST KEEP SCRUB-BING YOUR WAY THROUGH EVERY-THING!
TOMATO STAINS REALLY ARE STUB-BORN...
EVEN THE TASTIEST TOMATO STAINS AS SURELY AS BLOOD IF IT GETS SPLAT-TERED ALL OVER YOUR CLOTHES!
じゃぶ
SCRUBBA
じゃぶ
SCRUBBA
じゃぶ
SCRUBBA
IF WE DON'T MOVE FAST, IT'S STUCK FOR LIFE.
YOU KNOW, YOUR MAJESTY, I SEEM TO REMEMBER THAT AFTER LAST YEAR'S TOMATO KNIGHT WAS CROWNED...
YOU RETURNED TO THE CASTLE IMMEDIATE-LY AFTER GIVING YOUR BLESSING.
AT THIS RATE, I'LL BE LUCKY TO RETURN TODAY.
GO HURRY THAT GIRL ALONG, RUVAL.

Here's how to do laundry with washing soda today!
① SOAK THE CLOTHES IN A SOLUTION OF WASHING SODA (MAGIC POWDER HYPER) DISSOLVED IN WATER, THEN SCRUB WITH A BAR OF SOAP.
※ Soak for anywhere between three hours to overnight.
THE SOAP OF THIS WORLD IS A SIMPLE ADDITIVE-FREE VARIETY THAT'S GENTLE ON THE SKIN, BUT IT DOESN'T HAVE QUITE ENOUGH ALKALINITY TO SCRUB THINGS CLEAN.
IF YOU FIND YOURSELF IN A SIMILAR SITUATION, THE BEST THING IS TO PRETREAT YOUR CLOTHING IN AN ALKALINE SOLUTION TO HELP LIFT DIRT.
ADDITIVE-FREE SOAP IS SUITABLE FOR CLEANING FANCIER CLOTHES TOO, LIKE SILK AND FUR!
pH⑦
Standard Magic Powder
Baking Soda
PH 8.2 SUPER-LOW ALKALINITY
MIX BAKING SODA AND WASHING SODA TO CREATE SODIUM SESQUICARBONATE!
Super Magic Powder
Sodium Sesquicarbonate
PH 9.8 LOW ALKALINITY
Hyper Magic Powder
Washing Soda (sodium carbonate)
PH 11.2 ALKALINE
NOW!
HYPER POWDER (WASHING SODA!) IS SUPER ALKALINE AND HARMFUL TO BARE SKIN. DON'T FORGET TO WEAR RUBBER GLOVES!
WHEN DID THEY START SELLING SAINT-STAMPED GLOVES, ANYWAY?
② FILL A WASHING TUB WITH WATER AND START SCRUBBING WITH A WASHING BOARD.
RIGHT AWAY!
ALL RIGHT.
LET'S GET CLEANING, EVERYONE!
YES, LADY SAINT!

SIGH...
I SUPPOSE I'LL HAVE THE TOMATO-SOILED CLOTHES BROUGHT HERE.
STAY HERE AND WASH THEM. AND DO NOTHING ELSE.
I'M IN SOLITARY CONFINE-MENT...
WOOOP
OH! THERE SHE IS!
LADY SAINT!
YOU'RE ALL RIGHT!
WE'VE BROUGHT WHAT NEEDS TO BE CLEANED~!
WE'LL HELP YOU WASH THEM.
PWOMF
YOU'LL NEED ALL THE EXTRA HANDS YOU CAN GET!
OKAY! MILIA, YOU'RE IN CHARGE OF RUNNING INFO.
COUNT ON ME!
SADEEN, CAN YOU CARRY THE LAUNDRY BACK AND FORTH...?
VERY WELL.
AND... WHERE'S RUVAL?
HUNH. NOWHERE TO BE FOUND.
OH WELL! LET'S GET START-ED!

FWOOSH
YOU EXCEL AT ADDING FUEL TO THE FIRE.

SADEEN'S MAGICAL EXPERTISE IS IN FORTIFYING HIS OWN STRENGTH, AND THAT ALONE.
STRIP HIM OF THAT AND HE BECOMES THOROUGHLY USELESS.
WHAT...?
HE DOESN'T LOOK CHECKED OUT AT ALL...
TH-THANK YOU, YOUR MAJESTY...
AARGH! IT'S ON YOUR CLOAK, TOO?!
TAKE IT OFF! HURRY! IT'S GOING TO STAIN!
LUNGE
NOT EVEN HIS MAJESTY IS SAFE FROM HER!
SHE'S A FORCE OF NATURE!

DIDN'T I TELL YOU NOT TO MAKE A SCENE?

FWUP
ACK!
FWUP
FWUP
FWUP
THIS IS BAD.
IF THEY KEEP THROWING THEIR CLOTHES AT ME...
I'LL BE BURIED ALIVE!
SHIIING

THE SAINT IS STRIPPING US!
SAKU-RA!
LET US BEAT A HASTY RETREAT, YOUR HIGH-NESS. WOULDN'T WANT YOU GETTING HURT.
NO! I HAVE TO PROTECT HER TOO!
THE SAINT IS HERE? WHERE?!
HEY! WAIT YOUR TURN!
LADY SAINT!
I'LL TAKE OFF MY CLOTHES TOO!
HERE'S MINE!
D-DON'T HURT THEM, SA-DEEN...!
BLOOD STAINS ARE EVEN HARDER TO GET OUT THAN TO-MATOES!
FREEZE

SORRY TO BREAK UP THE HAPPY MOMENT, BUT TOMATO STAINS ARE A RACE AGAINST TIME!
EVERYBODY TAKE OFF YOUR CLOTHES AND GET SCRUBBING! PRONTO!!
STUNNED
IS THAT THE SAINT?!
OH!
THAT'S THE SAINT! FROM THE PALACE! LOOK, I'VE GOT HER PICTURE RIGHT HERE!
LADY SAINT!!
GLAD TO HEAR IT! NOW STRIP!
I COULDN'T LIVE WITH-OUT YOUR BROOMS AND MAGIC POWDER.
WAAH!

HOW AM I SUPPOSED TO STAY MAD AFTER HEARING A SETUP LIKE THAT?
UGH, FINE. WIN YOUR TOMATO WAR, PROPOSE TO HER, AND GET THIS OVER WITH!
MAY I PRESENT THIS YEAR'S TOMATO KNIGHT!
CLAP
CLAP
CLAP
CONGRATULATIONS!
MAY YOU LIVE HAPPILY EVER AFTER!
SPLORCH
SQUIRM
SQUIRM
SQUIRM
SQUIRM
SQUIRM
SQUIRM
SO DIRTY. MUST CLEAN. SO DI
DIRTY. MUST CLEAN.

GLOWWW
BEHOLD, THE GAL-LANT LAD YOOONDER!
MARK THE DETER-MINED GAZE HE CAST HIS EYES UPOOON!
HE WILL ACCEPT NO LESS THAN THE MANTLE OF THE TOMATO KNIGHT...
AND SURELY HIS LAAADY EXPECTS HIM TO FIIIGHT!
MARK MY WORDS, ONE PARENT, EITHER HIS OR HERS, REJECTS THEIR INTENT, HOWEVER PUUURE...
THEY MEET IN SECRET; FROM PRYING EYES THEY HIDE.
HE SWEARS ON HIS HONOR TO BECOME THE TOMATO KNIGHT...
AND TO MAKE HER HIS BRIIIIDE.
HMM?
AH, BUT WHAT'S THIS?
THE SHADOW OF FEEEAR HANGING O'ER A LAAASS. OUR FAIR TOMATO QUEEN SHOWS HER HEARTSTRINGS, INVESTED IN THIIIS DRAMATIC SCEEENE!
DID HE JUST PULL HIS LUTE OUT OF THIN AIR?
IS THERE ANYTHING MAGIC CAN'T DO?
ぽん
AND THOSE FELLOWS LOBBING THEIR FRUIT SO CAREFUL-LYYY?
COM-RADES-IN-ARMS, SURELY BEEE.
KNOWING HIS NOBLE QUEST, THEY WILL GUIDE HIM TO VICTORY!
AH, THE BEAUTY OF COMRA-DERIIIE.

HOW CAN THEY HAVE SUCH A FILTHY EVENT AT A TIME LIKE THIS?!
WE NEED TO STOP THE--
SSST
THIS FESTIVAL IS THE HIGHLIGHT OF THEIR YEAR.
THEY HURL TOMATOES AT ONE ANOTHER AND THE LAST MAN STANDING IS CROWNED THE TOMATO KNIGHT.
HE ALONE IS GIVEN THE RIGHT TO ASK ANY MAID IN THE VILLAGE FOR HER HAND IN MARRIAGE.
RAAAAHHH!
'TIS A TRADITION NO PARENT WOULD REFUSE.
EWW!
SPLAT
NOT TO WORRY! THE MAID HERSELF HAS THE FINAL SAY.

RAAAAH!
EAT TOMATO PASTE!!
WHAT'S GOING ON?!
IS IT A RIOT?!
NO, NO. THIS IS PART OF THE FESTIVAL!
THE TRADITIONAL TOMATO-THROWING CONTEST.
HUH?
HIS MAJESTY'S ADDRESS IS THE SIGNAL TO BEGIN.
BUT CLEANING MAGIC IS SEALED ALL ACROSS THE DEMON KING'S REALM, ISN'T IT...?

AND EVERY YEAR, AS TRADITION, THE DEMON KING SAYS ONLY THIS AND NOT A WORD MORE!
AH HA HA HA HA!
THAT'S THE ONLY REASON HE'S HERE?!
BEING THE DEMON KING MUST BE... WEIRD.
I'M STARTING TO SEE WHY HE WAS SO CHECKED OUT...
HOW ANNOYING.
HURRAY!
YEAAAH!
SQUEE!
WOO-HOO!
KER-SPLAT
WHAT THE...?!

SHE MUST BE THIS YEAR'S TOMATO QUEEN.
SHE WILL OFFER HIS MAJESTY THE CREAM OF THIS YEAR'S HARVEST.
MM.
THE TOMATO HARVEST HAS BEEN GOOD THIS YEAR.

IS THAT RIGHT?
YOU HAVE THE *NERVE* TO BE A PICKY EATER, DO YOU?
WITH THAT HULKING BODY, I THOUGHT YOU'D EAT ANYTHING!
OH, STOP IT!
MILIA WIELDS HER WORDS LIKE A **WHIP** ON GUYS WHO DON'T FAWN OVER HER...
TAKE HOME A TOMATER UMBRELLA TODAY!
AND DON'T FORGET YOUR TOMATO SWIM-SUITS!
PEOPLE WHO CAN'T STAND RAW TOMATOES SAY IT'S A TEXTURE THING.
AND ANYONE ATTENDING HIS MAJ-ESTY TODAY WILL HAVE ***BUSHELS*** OF THEM SHOVED DOWN THEIR THROAT.
HOW LUCKY THAT YOU WERE ASSIGNED TO BE THE SAINT'S DETAIL, SIR SADEEN.
HUZZAH!
HIS MAJESTY HAS AR-RIVED!!
HIS MAJESTY THE DEMON KING!
LOOK THIS WAY, YOUR MAJ-ESTY!

FRESH TOMATO JUICE! GET YOUR FRESH-SQUEEZED TOMATO JUICE HERE!
YOU KNOW, I JUST NOTICED THAT FOODS ARE CALLED THE SAME THINGS HERE AS THEY ARE BACK HOME.
COME TRY OUR DELICIOUS TOMATO-LOADED PIZZA!
MAYBE THAT INTER-PRETATION ENCHANTMENT IS CONVERTING IT TO SOME-THING MY JAPANESE MIND CAN UNDERSTAND?
IT ALL LOOKS SO GOOD~!
GIDDY
GIDDY
TOMATO BUNS, TOMATO PUDDING? I WANT TO TRY IT ALL!
WHAT'S THE MATTER, SADEEN? DON'T YOU LIKE THEM?
ULP!
I CAN... STOMACH TOMATOES WHEN COOKED.
BUT NEVER RAW.

LONELY? WE ONLY JUST MET!
YOU'RE SUCH A SMOOTH-TALKER, RUVAL!
NOT LONELY, THEN. ♪
BUT I WILL SAY IT'S BEEN A TREAT TO SEE THE PALACE TURNED UPSIDE DOWN EVERY DAY SINCE YOUR COMING.
I EXPECT THE FUN IS ONLY JUST BEGINNING...
AND I EXPECT TO KEEP MY FRONT-ROW SEEEAT! ♪

THEY'VE MADE MUCH PROGRESS CLEARING AWAY THOSE MOUNTAINS OF ASH.
OWING TO SAINT SAKURA'S STAMPED CLEANING RELICS, I'M SURE. ♪
WHAT'S THAT?
IT APPEARS THEY'RE GATHERING THE ASH INTO PILES.
DO YOU THINK THEY WOULD DISAPPEAR IF *I* CLEANED THEM UP?
WHY, FOR ALL WE KNOW, THEY COULD VANISH THE MOMENT THE WITCH'S HEX IS BROKEN!
YEAH...
HOPEFULLY.
THE SEARCH PARTY HASN'T REPORTED ANY LEADS ON WHERE THE CRUX OF THE CURSE IS HIDING, THOUGH...
HMM. AND WHAT A MIXED BAG THAT IS.
FOR MY PART, I WILL CERTAINLY BE LONELY WITHOUT YOU.

DON'T CAUSE A SCENE. I WON'T PUT UP WITH IT.
THESE THREE CAN KEEP ME IN CHECK.
I'LL JUST CHECK THINGS OUT WHILE KEEPING A LOW PROFILE!
THIS VEXES ME FOR SOME REASON...
FINE... I'LL ALLOW IT.
THANK YOU, YOUR MAJESTY!
COME TO THINK OF IT, I HAVEN'T STEPPED FOOT OUTSIDE THE CASTLE SINCE I ARRIVED HERE...
ANYWAY, THERE'S ALWAYS A MOUNTAIN OF TRASH AFTER EVERY FESTIVAL!
I CAN TOTALLY STICK AROUND TO CLEAN IT UP!

I DON'T WANT PEOPLE TO FUSS OVER ME AS THE SAINT.
I JUST WANT TO SEE HOW NORMAL DEMONS LIVE OUTSIDE THE PALACE.
GASP
CAN'T I SPLIT OFF FROM HIS MAJESTY AND DO MY OWN THING?
VERY WELL. SADEEN, YOU WILL ESCORT HER.
I'LL GO TOO!
?
NO. IT'S NOTH-ING.
IT WILL BE DONE.
HMPT!
WON-DERFUL!
I SHALL ACCOMPANY THE LADY SAINT AS WELL!
HEY! YOU CAN'T GO IN THERE!
BURST
YOU PRO-MISED YOU WOULD ONLY LISTEN IN!

A NEARBY VILLAGE IS CELEBRATING THEIR TOMATO HARVEST WITH A FESTIVAL.
HIS MAJESTY IS, BY CUSTOM, EXPECTED TO ATTEND.
FLUTTER
A FESTI-VAL?!
OOOH, CAN I COME?
I DON'T SEE WHY NOT. YOU COULD USE A DAY OFF YOURSELF.
THE LIES YOU TELL.
I'LL NOT HAVE IT SAID THAT THE DEMON KING TREATS HIS PEOPLE UNFAIRLY.
I SHALL SEND WORD THAT THE LADY SAINT WILL BE ACCOMPANY-ING HIS MAJESTY.
OH!
NO, I DON'T MEAN LIKE THAT.

IT IS TIME FOR TOMORROW'S FITTING.
FITTING FOR WHAT?
AH. THAT.
HOW ANNOY-ING.
LIKE IT OR NOT, SIRE, YOU KNOW THE RULES ON PUBLIC APPEAR-ANCES.
WHAT'S GOING ON TOMOR-ROW?

I'M TAKATSUKI SAKURA. AND WITH HIS MAJESTY, THE DEMON KING'S PERMISSION (HIS WORDS WERE, "YOU'RE TOO TINY TO BOTHER ME UNDER-FOOT")...
GA-KLINK
MY NEW DUTY IS TO KEEP HIS ROOM NEAT AND TIDY.
TUNK
SHELF
KEEP
YOU'D THINK IT'D BE LIKE CLEANING A ROOM WITH A PORCELAIN DOLL HAP-HAZARDLY THROWN ON THE BED...
AND IF HE WOULDN'T OPEN HIS MOUTH, YOU'D BE RIGHT. PROBLEM IS, HE DOES. OFTEN.
ENOUGH RACKET.
I DO NOT CARE IF YOU CLEAN MY ROOM, SO LONG AS YOU DO IT QUIETLY.
I'D BE DONE ALREADY IF YOU DIDN'T LET IT GET THIS BAD, YOUR MAJESTY!
YOUR MAJESTY.

IS SHE CRYING FOR HER FAMILY? OR IS IT THE BOOK?
KNOWING HER... COULD BE BOTH.
"I don't have time to cry even if I wanted to."
WHO IS THIS "KAEDE"?
SHMACK
MY LITTLE BROTHER.
SHMACK
IT TAKES SKILL TO ANSWER IN YOUR SLEEP.
HMPH.
YOUNG WOMEN ARE SO CARELESS.
SQUEEZE

SO SHE DOES CRY FROM LONELI-NESS.
NOD
NOD
NO. SHE'S SLEEPING!
MOM, DAD...
HECK, EVEN KAEDE...
COULD YOU TELL THE LIBRARY I'M SORRY MY BOOKS ARE TWO WEEKS OVER-DUE...?
FLOAT
AH...

ALL RIGHT! THAT OUGHTA DO IT FOR THE INNER COURT-YARD.
THANK YOU FOR YOUR HELP, LADY SAINT.
WHEW... THIS CLEANING MAGIC IS HARD WORK!
SAKURA?
MOM...
DAD...

Chapter 4 ✧ The Pitter-Pat of the Demon King's Awakening Heart

OHH ...
THIS IS ALMOST SCARIER THAN ANY GHOST...
ぽすん…
CATCH
IT COULD BE.
I SHOULD HAVE THOUGHT HARDER BEFORE DRAWING UP THAT SAKURA SIGIL FOR HIM...
HUNH. HE SMILED...
SHORTLY AFTER THAT...
CHATTER
CHATTER
WE'RE MAKING A KILLING, LADY SAINT!
PLEASE STOP!!
The Hot New Item, Produced by Lehaye
Magic Powder
★ STANDARD (SODIUM BICARBONATE/BAKING SODA)
★ SUPER (SODIUM SESQUICARBONATE)
★ HYPER (SODIUM CARBONATE/WASHING SODA)
Now on sale!
TRUST THE SIGIL OF THE SAINT!
Chapter 3/End

HANG ON.
IS THIS AN AD?!
"THE SAINT'S MAGIC POWDER, NOW ON SALE!"
THAT'S WHAT IT SAYS, SAKURA.
THE SAINT'S MAGIC POWDER? WHAT THE HECK IS... WAIT.
IS THAT SUPPOSED TO BE BAKING SODA?!
(Hyper)
(Super)
(Standard)
THEY DIDN'T HAVE TO GIVE IT A CRAZY NAME LIKE *THAT!*
IT'S ALMOST PHOTO-REALISTIC!
IT ALSO SAYS, "COMES WITH A LIMITED-EDITION PICTURE OF THE SAINT. WHILE SUPPLIES LAST."
JEEZ~!! NOW I'M BLUSH-ING!!
DON'T USE YOUR COPY MAGIC FOR *THIS!*
LEHAYE HAS YOU IN HIS CROSS-HAIRS.
HE'S A SALESMAN, AFTER ALL.
ONCE HE SEES POTENTIAL IN A PRODUCT, HE DIGS IN AND WON'T LET GO.
NYA-OW?!
GET A HOLD OF YOURSELF, SAKURA!

THE DEMON KING IS LAZY. NO TWO WAYS ABOUT IT. BUT HE'S SURPRISINGLY KIND, TOO.
HMM... I COULD ALWAYS USE TEA LEAVES OR LAY DOWN NEWS-PAPER IF HE DOESN'T LIKE THE DUST...
LADY SAINT!
I HAVE LAST NIGHT'S EVENING NEWS HERE IF YOU'D LIKE IT!
THANKS.
WHAT'S IT CALLED? DEMON'S GENERATION?
THAT'S RIGHT. WE CALL IT THE DEGENERATE FOR SHORT.
YEAH, I'M NOT SHORTENING THAT.
WHY DO YOU WANT TO GET IT WET AND SCATTER THE PIECES ALL OVER THE FLOOR?
RRRIP RRRIP RRRIP RRRIP
THAT WAY, THE DUST AND DIRT WILL CLING TO THE DAMP NEWSPAPER, AND I CAN SWEEP WITH-OUT KICKING UP ANY CLOUDS.

A MERE CLEAN-ING?!
COME ON.
CLEANING IS SUPER IMPORTANT! IT'S GOOD FOR YOUR BODY AND YOUR MIND!
PEOPLE MIGHT OVERSELL ME BY SAYING I'M SOME SAINT...
BUT IF MY CLEANING KNOW-HOW CAN BE OF ANY USE...
THEN I'D LIKE TO USE IT FOR YOU, YOUR MAJESTY.

YEAH... I AM.
BESIDES.
I DON'T HAVE TIME TO CRY EVEN IF I WANTED TO.
THIS PALACE IS A FILTHY WRECK!
SWEEP
SWEEP
SWEEP
SWEEP
STOP SWEEPING OVER THERE. YOU'RE KICKING UP DUST.
AND IT VEXES ME TO SEE YOU SCUTTLING ABOUT.
THEN GO SOME-WHERE ELSE AND LET ME CLEAN IN PEACE.
WHY MUST I LEAVE MY OWN CHAMBERS FOR A MERE CLEANING?

SLIDE
IS THAT ALL? HERE.
THERE'S A HIDDEN DOOR BACK HERE!
IS THIS YOUR STORAGE AREA?!
LOOK AROUND. SOMETHING IN HERE OBVIOUSLY FELL OVER.
OF COURSE IT WOULD! THAT'S BECAUSE EVERYTHING'S PILED SO HAP-HAZARDLY.
I REALLY HATE SUDDEN NOISES, SO WHENEVER I HEAR ONE, I CALL IT A GHOST.
I KNOW IT'S A STORAGE CLOSET, YOUR MAJESTY, BUT YOU SHOULD REALLY KEEP IT TIDY.
SO, THE GIRL WHO CAME FROM ANOTHER WORLD, LIVES IN AN UNFAMILIAR CASTLE, AND CHEERFULLY CLEANS IT WITHOUT SHEDDING A TEAR OR A WORD OF COMPLAINT...
IS AFRAID OF GHOSTS.

KRASSHHH
BANG
YEEK!!
GH-GHOST?!
NO GHOST WOULD SHOW ITS FACE IN THE DEMON KING'S CHAMBERS.
B-BUT I...
I HEARD A NOISE! THERE WASN'T ANYTHING THERE, BUT I HEARD IT!!
CALM DOWN. TELL ME WHERE IT CAME FROM.
THE WALL...

YOU KNOW... WATCHING A GORGEOUS DEMON KING CRAFT MOUNTAIN AFTER MOUNTAIN OF BROOMS AND DUSTERS AFTER WORK IN HIS GORGEOUS ROOM PAINTS A REALLY SURREAL PICTURE...
THUD THUD THUD THUD
WAIT, WAIT! PLEASE SEPARATE THEM INTO CATEGO-RIES!
BROOMS GO OVER HERE, AND DUSTERS OVER HERE!
SWISH
SWISH
HMM-HMM-HMM~

SORRY TO BUG YOU WHEN YOU ARE CLEARLY NOT HAVING A GOOD TIME...
BUT COULD YOU WHIP ME UP AN EXTRA PAIR OF RUBBER GLOVES WHEN YOU'RE DONE?
WHAT? GOT A PROBLEM?
......
ZWOOP
THANK YOU SO MUCH!
ALL RIGHT!
THE THICKNESS AND THE FIT ARE EXACTLY THE SAME AS THE ORIG-INAL!
AS EXPECTED OF THE DEMON KING WITH ENDLESS MP!
ZWOOP
ZWOOP
ZWOOP
ZWOOP
ZWOOP
ZWOOP
ZWOOP
ZWOOP
ZWOOP

MAGIC IS WEIRD.
AN INFERIOR COPY CANNOT REPLICATE THE SAINT'S OWN MAGIC, YOU KNOW.
THAT IS WHY YOU ARE THE ONLY MAN FOR THIS JOB.
AT ANY RATE, NEED I REMIND YOU WE ARE ONLY IN THIS MESS BECAUSE YOU SO COLDLY REJECTED THE ADVANCES OF A CERTAIN WITCH?
I WOULD ASK YOU TO MAKE AMENDS BY GIVING HER YOUR AID.
I'VE NEVER HEARD OF A DEMON KING WITH SO LITTLE AMBITION.
BUT IT SEEMS PRETTY PEACEFUL AROUND HERE, SO THAT'S PROBABLY FINE... RIGHT?
AFTER ALL, IF SOME DEMON KING STARTED RAMPAGING WITH HIS SIGHTS SET ON GLOBAL DOMINATION, THE WORLD WOULD PLUNGE INTO CHAOS.
I'LL RETURN LATER TO RETRIEVE THEM.
ZWIP
ZWOOP
UM... YOUR MAJ-ESTY?

AH, BUT HIS MAJESTY COULDN'T MAKE APPEARANCES EVERY DAY, COULD HE? THE COMMON FOLK WOULD BEGIN TO TAKE HIM FOR GRANTED.
INSTEAD, WE TEASE THE PEOPLE. GIVE THEM A LITTLE TASTE, AND THEN, GASP! THERE HE IS!
ZZZ...
A LITTLE STAGING IS NECESSARY FOR EVERY EVENT, WHICH IS WHY WE HOLD COURT ONLY TWICE A MONTH.
IT'S AN ACT.
HIS MAJESTY THE BUSINESSMAN AND HIS PRODUCER. WHAT ELSE DID I EXPECT?
PSST...
HEY, MILIA? DOES HE REALLY HAVE BUCKETS OF MP, JUST LIKE YOU SAID...?
OH, IT'S TRUE.
CAN'T YOU TELL, SAKURA?
IT SENDS TINGLES UP MY SPINE!
I CAN'T TELL. SURE, HIS AURA IS INTIMIDATING...
BUT MAYBE IT'S A SENSATION THAT ONLY OTHER DEMONS CAN CATCH.

OOO-KAY...
SO IT WAS A PEACEFUL TRANSITION!
WHEN THE PREVIOUS DEMON KING LEARNED OF HIS MAJESTY'S OVERWHELMING MAGIC, HE RAISED HIM AS HIS SUCCESSOR.
I UNWILLINGLY INHERITED THE THRONE, BUT I HAVE NO DESIRE TO WORK.
SO, IN EXCHANGE FOR KEEPING UP APPEARANCES TO THE PUBLIC...
I'M ALLOWED TO DO AS I PLEASE OUTSIDE OF OFFICIAL BUSINESS.
WOW. HE ISN'T INTO THIS DEMON KING THING, IS HE?
TO THINK DEMON KING IS JUST A TITLE IN NAME...
......
CLAP

WHERE DID THAT NOBILITY FROM BEFORE GO...?
IS HE EVEN THE SAME PERSON?
NOW HE'S JUST LAZING AROUND... LAZING IN ENNUI.
WAIT, SO THE DEMON KING IS SCOUTED?
YOU DIDN'T, LIKE, DEFEAT THE LAST ONE AND STEAL HIS CROWN?
DO I *LOOK* LIKE I'D WASTE TIME ON WARS OF SUCCESSION?
HE MAKES IT SOUND LIKE HE'D RATHER NOT SHOW UP AT ALL.
I WAS SCOUTED TO BECOME THE DEMON KING AND AGREED BASED SOLELY ON THE PROMISE OF LIVING LAVISHLY OFF OF MY PASSIVE INCOME.
I WORK TOO MUCH AS IT IS.

WAIT... IS THAT WHY I KEEP GETTING HOLES IN THE CLOTHES AND RUBBER GLOVES THAT MILIA DUPLICATED FOR ME...?
AND WHY ARE YOU BACK IN CAT FORM?
BE-CAUSE I'M OUT OF MP!
NYAAAAAH!!
EXCUSE ME FOR NOT BEING A SPECIAL-IST!
IF IT'S A PERFECT COPY YOU WANT, THEN GO SEE *HIM!*
YOU WANT *ME* TO SHOULDER THE BURDEN OF EXTRA WORK? DON'T BE A FOOL.
HMPH.

WELL, HOW ABOUT THIS?
SCRITCH
SCRITCH
I WAS NAMED AFTER A FLOWER THAT BLOOMS IN THE SPRING IN THE LAND I COME FROM.
I SEE... THE SAKURA BLOSSOM, THEN.
WE LACK SUCH A FLOWER IN THIS WORLD. I'M SURE IT WILL MAKE A FINE FAMILY CREST FOR YOU.
FWWSH
I SHALL TAKE THESE TO A DUPLICATION SPECIALIST AND HAVE COPIES MASS-PRODUCED POST-HASTE.
A SPECIAL-IST?
DUPLICATION MAGIC IS COMMONPLACE HERE, BUT IT TENDS TO BETRAY ITS USER'S ABILITY... OR LACK THEREOF.
IF A USER WITH A SMALL MAGIC FOUNT USES IT, IT WILL ONLY YIELD INFERIOR COPIES.

I'VE MADE A MOMENTOUS DISCOVERY!
PLEASE MARK THESE WITH YOUR SAINTLY SIGIL!
DUSTER
BROOM
I'M SORRY. MY WHAT?
HEH!
WHEN THE PALACE HANDS TOOK UP THE DUSTER AND THE BROOM YOU USED, SAKURA, THEY WERE ABLE TO VANQUISH THE UNCLEAN ASH JUST AS YOU DID!
SORCERY!
I INTEND TO DUPLICATE AND DISTRIBUTE COPIES TO HOUSEHOLDS ACROSS THE KINGDOM AS RELICS BRANDED WITH THE SAINT'S HOLY SEAL.
WE CAN'T EXPECT YOU TO CLEAN UP ALL OF THE ASH IN THE REALM BY YOURSELF, COULD WE?
AWW...
URGH... YEAH, I GUESS YOU'RE RIGHT...

YOU'RE SO CUTE, MILIA!
ちやほや GUSH
ちやほや GUSH
OF COURSE! I'M SAINT SAKURA'S LOVELY LADY-IN-WAITING.
AND AT SUCH A YOUNG AGE! GOOD FOR YOU!
HEY!!
I'M SEVENTEEN, THANKS!
YOU MEAN THERE'S ONLY ONE YEAR BETWEEN US?!
NO WAY!
HUH?!
YOU'RE SIXTEEN, MILIA?!
I'M OLDER THAN YOU ARE!
I'M EIGHTEEN!
ARE YOU KIDDING ME?!
UH-OH..
PLUCK
HANG ON, HOW CAN YOU TURN INTO A HUMAN, ANYWAY?
BRILLIANT DEMON BEASTS, SUCH AS MYSELF, CAN USE SHAPE-SHIFTING MAGIC.
KNOCK KNOCK
SAKURA?
MAY I BEG A MOMENT OF YOUR TIME?

COULD THAT BE THE FAMOUS HOUSE-KEEPING SAINT?!
SHE'S LOVELY!
POOF
WHAT THE--?!
YOU CAN TURN INTO A HUMAN, MILIA?!
HE'S JUST AS BAD AS THEY ARE.
HEH.

AND WITH THE HOUSEKEEPING SAINT HERE, THE DEMON KING'S AUTHORITY IS, NATURALLY, SECURE!
HENCE...
THE MOUNTAIN OF OFFER-INGS OVER THERE.
WHOA!
EVEN THOUGH *YOU* DID ALL OF THE HARD WORK AND HE DIDN'T LIFT A FINGER!
MYEW-HEW!
YOU'RE REALLY HARD ON HIS MAJ-ESTY, HUH?
I'M NOT INTO EGOTIS-TICAL LOUTS.
NYA HA HA!
NYA HA HA!
OH DEAR.
THOSE TWO...
WHAT ARE THEY WHISPERING ABOUT BACK THERE?
IF THESE COMMONERS SPOT THEM, I'LL NEVER HEAR THE END OF IT...
GO GIGGLE SOME-WHERE ELSE. UGH.

HIS... WHAT?
OH, IT'S LEHAYE. HE TAPS INTO DEMONS' *INEXHAUSTIBLE* LOVE FOR ALL THINGS BEAUTIFUL...
ALL HAIL THE KING!
STEERING PUBLIC OPINION WITH COMMENTS LIKE, "HIS MAJESTY IS SO BEAUTIFUL THAT HE ENCHANTED A WITCH FROM ANOTHER WORLD!"
"YET HE IS SO NOBLE THAT HE WOULD NOT FALL TO HER TEMPTATION!"
THE POWER OF SUG-GESTION, REALLY.
No demon king could break a curse cast by a witch from another world, no ma
miracle in all the land is His Majesty himself!
But you needn't worry! Salvation shall come to us in time. After all, the greatest
AND THEY BOUGHT IT? JUST LIKE THAT?
WELL, YOU'RE HERE NOW, AREN'T YOU?
SO IT ALL WORKED OUT IN THE END.

WOW...
EVEN FROM THIS DISTANCE, HIS REGAL BEARING IS ALMOST INTIMIDAT-ING!
WELL, DUH. HE'S THE DEMON KING.
HUH?
HANG ON. THAT WITCH CAST HER ANTI-CLEANING HEX...
TO GET BACK AT THE DEMON KING, RIGHT?
HOW COME HIS APPROVAL RATING HASN'T DROPPED AT ALL?
WE HAVE HIS *INFINITELY* GIFTED PRODUCER TO THANK FOR THAT.

ARE THEY ALL DEMONS?!
IT'S A WONDER THEY CAN ALL SPEAK THE SAME LANGUAGE.
FROM WHAT I'VE LEARNED, DEMONS TEND TO WORSHIP AND ADORE ANYTHING BEAUTIFUL.
THAT'S WHY HIS HANDSOME HIGHNESS THE DEMON KING IS SUCH A ROCK STAR HERE.
HOLY--! DOES HE HAVE A FAN CLUB?!
YOUR MAJ-ESTY!
DESPITE THE DIFFICULTIES POSED BY THE UNCLEAN ASH, OUR TOMATO FESTIVAL IS STILL RIGHT ON SCHEDULE FOR THIS YEAR.
WOULD YOU GRACE US WITH YOUR PRES-ENCE?

TO BE HONEST, I'M A LITTLE SCARED.
PEEK
BUT CLEANING IS FUN...AND I WANT TO LEARN MORE ABOUT THIS WORLD, TOO.
HE HASN'T HELD COURT IN HALF A MONTH!
I DO WISH HE'D MAKE MORE TIME FOR AUDIENCES.
OH, JUST LOOK AT HIM! ISN'T HIS MAJESTY GORGEOUS?

Couldn't we just draw a new one?
AH...
While that is possible in theory, we cannot guarantee that the circle would connect back to where you came from.
In the worst event, you might be stuck in an endless loop, rolling from one world to the next. I dare say you wouldn't enjoy that.
HA HA!
No! I do **not** want to be a contestant on an episode of ***The Great Isekai Road-trip!***
As for the witch, she returned to your world while sending you to ours.
Nooooo!
At any rate, once we find a way to keep the Unclean Ash from falling, we should once again have access to the magic circle to send you home.
And to do that...
I HAVE TO FIND THE CRUX OF THE CURSE THAT THE WITCH HID SOMEWHERE IN THIS WORLD.
SOON, IF I CAN...
LET'S GO AL-READY!

YOU'VE BEEN WORKING FOR FIVE DAYS STRAIGHT NOW! NEED I REMIND YOU THAT YOU'RE THE HOUSEKEEPING SAINT?
TEACH YOUR METHODS OF MAGIC-FREE CLEANING TO THE SERVANTS, AND THEY'LL HAPPILY HANDLE THE REST.
OH, IT'S FINE.
REALLY!
I LIKE TO KEEP MYSELF BUSY ANYWAY.
DON'T WORRY, I'LL STILL MAKE TIME FOR HIS MAJESTY'S COURT.
AFTER ALL, KEEPING BUSY HELPS KEEP ME DISTRACTED.
You wish to find a way back to your homeland?
IT'S BEEN FIVE DAYS SINCE I CAME TO THIS WORLD.
That would be... difficult.
The magic circle which transported you here in the first place, located in Manak Castle, has been re-buried by the Unclean Ash.

ANOTHER MASTER-PIECE, CHEF!
IF YOU'LL EXCUSE ME, I MUST SEE TO THE NEXT ITEM ON MY AGENDA.
SURE! I'VE GOTTA RUN ANYWAY.
I'M GOING TO GO CHECK OUT THE REST OF THE PALACE!
AHA!
YOU CAN'T HIDE FROM ME, DIRT!
BOFF
BOFF
BOFF
BOFF
BOFF
I SEE YOU TOO, DUST!
HON-ESTLY, SAKURA, NOT AGAIN!
WHY DO YOU INSIST ON CARRYING YOUR CLEANING SUPPLIES WITH YOU?
AREN'T YOU EXHAUST-ED FROM SCRUBBING THE CASTLE FROM MORN-ING UNTIL NIGHT?

YOUR BREAKFAST, LADY.
WE DO HOPE YOU'LL FAVOR US AGAIN TODAY!
OH!
S-SURE...
I'M NOT A SAINT, THOUGH.
IN JAPAN, I'M A TOTALLY AVERAGE HIGH SCHOOL STUDENT! JUST CALL ME SAKURA, OKAY?
NONSENSE, SAKURA! IF I AM GOING TO BE YOUR FAMILIAR...
THEN *SAINT* IS A FAR BETTER TITLE TO HAVE THAN *AVERAGE HI-SHULE STUDENT!*
JUST SO, PRINCESS MILIA.
I SEE WE AGREE FOR ONCE, LEHAYE.
WHATEVER. I'M HUNGRY.
HRM...
IT'S BETTER TO OVER-EMPHASIZE YOUR SAINTLINESS. IT APPEALS TO THE COMMON PEOPLE.
AND IT WILL HELP DISCOURAGE ATTACKS FROM ANY ILL-TEMPERED DEMONS.
ULTIMATELY, IT'S FOR YOUR OWN SAFETY.
BUT IF YOU PREFER SOMETHING OTHER THAN YOUR UNIFORM, WE HAVE NO SHORTAGE OF DRESSES.
I'LL STICK WITH MY SCHOOL UNIFORM, THANKS.

BUT HERE IN THE DEMON KING'S REALM, CLEANING MAGIC IS SEALED AWAY THANKS TO SOME WITCH'S CURSE.
UNTIL THAT POINT, THE CITIZENS HAD ALL DEPENDED ON CLEANING MAGIC TO KEEP EVERYTHING TIDY...
CLUTTER
SO THE PLACE WAS FILTHY BY THE TIME I GOT HERE!
THEY WERE WEIRDLY IMPRESSED WITH MY CLEANING SKILLS, AND NOW...
YOUR PARDON, HOUSE-KEEPING SAINT.
KA-KLNK KA-KLNK KA-KLNK
THEY CALL ME THE HOUSE-KEEPING SAINT. HEY, I DIDN'T ASK THEM TO!
WHY, THOSE ARE ALL VESTMENTS OF THE OTHER-WORLDLY SAINT SAKURA.
THIS IS A WORLD WHERE EVERY-ONE USES MAGIC.
MILIA USED HER DUPLICATION MAGIC TO CREATE REPLICAS OF THE CLOTHING YOU ORIGINALLY WORE HERE.
'TWAS SIMPLE, REALLY.
POP POP POP POP POP POP

SAKURA! RISE AND SHINE!
KITTY PUNCH!
STARTLE
GH- GH- GH- GHOST !!
WAKE UP ALREADY! HIS MAJESTY IS HOLDING COURT TODAY, AND WE'RE GOING TO SPY ON HIM.
YOU SHOULD SEE THE LINE ALREADY! NOW GO THROW SOME CLOTHES ON.
OH, ALL RIGHT.
PHEW...
IT WAS JUST A DREAM...
CLICK
UH...
MILIA?! MY CLOTHES MULTIPLIED!!
SAKURA?
PAR- DON THE INTRUSION. IS AUGHT AMISS?
LEHAYE? WHAT HAPPENED HERE...?

Ooooh, there she is!
That's what happens when you don't clean up!
BUH-THUMP!
EVER SINCE THEN, I'VE HAD A CLEANING OBSESSION THAT'S LASTED OVER TEN YEARS.
AH HA HA!
HONEY, STOP...
EVENTUALLY, I REALIZED THAT WAS MY MOM'S WAY OF GETTING ME TO CLEAN MY ROOM...
BUT BY THAT POINT, CLEANING WAS ALREADY THE LOVE OF MY LIFE.
SST
SA... KU... RAAA!

WHEN I WAS A KID...
I CAUGHT THIS SHOW ON TV ABOUT GHOST HUNTING.
AND, WELL...IT TRAUMA-TIZED ME FOR LIFE.
Its owner's ghost haunts this hoarding nightmare!
BA-DMP
BA-DMP
BA-DMP
Sakura...
You know what ghosts love? Dirty rooms.
REACH

Chapter 3 ✦ The Saint's Miracles Are Cherry Blossom-Approved!

Chapter 2/End

SHE SLEPT AND SLEPT, AND WHEN I WENT TO SEE WHETHER SHE WAS AWAKE...
SHE LUNGED AT ME WITH DESPERATION IN HER EYES.
AS THOUGH...
PROTECTING ME FROM SOMETHING.
AS FAR AS THE DEMON REALM IS CONCERNED, MAJESTY, SHE IS A BONA FIDE SAINT.
ALBEIT... A RATHER PINT-SIZED ONE.
A PINT-SIZED SAINT IS STILL A SAINT.
AND DOES THAT NOT WORK IN OUR FAVOR?
SHE IS A METICULOUS GIRL WHO APPRECIATES TIDINESS.
SO, THEN, LET US PUT HER TO WORK.

Once she awakens, give her gold for her journey and get her out of the palace.
No, Your Majesty!
There is something special about her.
MWEE HEE.

What small, filthy creature is this?
Your Majesty...
this is no creature.
It's a young woman from another world.
You see? If you wipe her face, she's quite comely.
SCRUB SCRUB
After the last one, what damage will **this** female creature do to my kingdom?
Turn it into a swamp?

LONG LIVE THE SAINT!
LADY SAINT!
YOUR SAINT-LINESS!
SHE ADAPTED QUICKLY, DIDN'T SHE.
LIKE THE WITCH, SHE HAS COURAGE...
BUT I'VE NEVER SEEN THE PALACE HANDS SPURN THEIR KING IN FAVOR OF AN OTHER-WORLDER.
LADY SAINT!
SAINT SAKURA!
THE HOUSE-KEEPING SAINT...

Whoa... Look at that!
It's clean and shiny!
That's right, Kaede! Isn't it cool?
Yeah! Just like magic.
YOU KNOW... I CAN LIVE WITH THIS.

じゅわ〜っ
FIZZZ
SHE DID THAT WITH VINEGAR AND BAKING SODA?!
THAT GOT RID OF THE SLIME AND THE SMELL!
CAUSED BY BACTERIA!
How to remove slime from a drain
① REMOVE ANY PHYSICAL BLOCKAGE.
② DUMP IN PLENTY OF BAKING SODA, THEN POUR VINEGAR OVER TOP.
➡ THE ALKALINITY OF THE SODA AND ACIDIC VINEGAR INTERACT TO FORM BUBBLES, LIFTING THE DIRT TO THE SURFACE.
......
THEY'RE MAGIC BUBBLES!
THE LADY SAINT'S MIRACLES ARE UN-STOPPABLE!!
IT'S NOT A MIRACLE. IT'S SCIENCE!
HERE, GIVE IT A TRY.
I CLEANED IT WITH BAKING SODA ALL BY MYSELF!
LONG LIVE THE SAINT!
SHE'S SAVED US WITH HER OTHER-WORLDLY MAGIC!
THANK YOU, LADY SAINT!

LADY SAINT! NOW THE DRAIN IS CLOGGED!
DID HIS MAJESTY FORESEE THIS...?
COULD YOU WASH THESE TOO?
AND THIS, PLEASE!
AND THESE!
WHAT A STRANGE WORLD I'VE LANDED IN.
BUT...
Are you looking for new cleaning guides again? That's so you.
Did you know that Sakura made all of the cleaning solutions we used today?
No way! You can do that?
They don't call her the Super Cleaner for nothing!
She gets special recognition all the time during the morning assemblies too!
We couldn't match her if we tried.

OOOOOH!
THEY REACT WITH SO MUCH SURPRISE, EVEN THOUGH THESE CLEANING TECH-NIQUES HAVE BEEN PASSED DOWN FOR YEARS.
AND IF I THOUGHT THE KITCHEN WAS BAD, THEN THE WHOLE PALACE...
HECK, THE ENTIRE KINGDOM IS PROBABLY A CESSPOOL OF FILTH IF IT HASN'T HAD A GOOD CLEANING IN SO LONG!
HEH!
APPEAR-ANCES AREN'T OUR SAINT'S ONLY FORTE. TRULY, IT'S HER IMPRESSIVE WORK ETHIC TAKING CENTER STAGE!

どやっ
SMUG
I KNEW THAT HAD TO BE IT.
THANKS FOR THE GREAT MEAL TODAY!
MY COMPLIMENTS TO THE CHEF.
D'AWW!
THEY *WANT* TO TAKE GOOD CARE OF THE THINGS THEY TREASURE, JUST LIKE WE DO BACK IN MY WORLD.
YOU'VE SAVED ME, LADY SAINT!
THOSE POTS AND PANS WERE COLLECTING RUST FOR OVER SIX MONTHS...
I THOUGHT FOR SURE I'D LIVE TO SEE THE CROWN JEWELS OF OUR KITCHEN RUINED!
YOU HAVE NO IDEA HOW SCARED I WAS!
THEY DIDN'T KNOW THE WAY, THAT'S ALL.

FIRST THINGS FIRST!
THE SALT!
IF YOU THROW SOME SALT INTO AN IRON PAN, DRY ROAST IT, THEN GIVE IT A QUICK SCRUB, THE BURNED BITS WILL FALL RIGHT OFF.
OOOH!
HMM... REGULAR OLD BAKING SODA ISN'T GOING TO CUT IT FOR THIS ONE.
SPOOOOSH
HAR-RUMPH!
WASHING SODA SHOULD DO THE TRICK, THOUGH.
YOU'LL NEVER GET THAT ONE CLEAN WITHOUT MAGIC.
Cleaning a burned pot using baking soda and washing soda.
DRY ROAST SALT IN AN IRON PAN TO MAKE THE SCORCH MARKS FALL OFF.
Aluminum
Vinegar
Stainless steel
Iron
Salt
Baking Soda
FOR STAINLESS STEEL PANS, BRING A SOLUTION OF WATER AND BAKING SODA TO A BOIL TO LIFT THE SCORCH MARKS.
※ FOR ALUMINUM PANS, BRING A SOLUTION OF WATER AND VINEGAR TO A BOIL AND SCRUB WITH AN ORGANIC SPONGE.
HOW CAN BAKING SODA GET THINGS CLEAN, ANYWAY?
BAKING SODA HAS COARSE PARTICLES AND IS ABRASIVE, SO IT CAN BE USED FOR POLISHING.
IT'S ALSO ALKALINE, SO IT CAN ALSO NEUTRALIZE AND REMOVE ACIDIC GREASE AND SCORCH MARKS.
HEATING BAKING SODA (SODIUM BICARBONATE) TURNS IT INTO WASHING SODA (SODIUM CARBONATE), WHICH HAS A HIGHER PH AND IS MORE ALKALINE. HOWEVER, ITS PARTICLES ARE TOO SMALL TO USE AS AN ABRASIVE AGENT.
CLEANING IS ALL A MATTER OF CHEMISTRY!
BAKING POWDER IS FULL OF ADDITIVES, SO IT'S NO GOOD FOR CLEANING!!
ALL RIGHT...
WHAT DO YOU HAVE TO SAY TO THIS?

SAINT?! PHOOEY!
THOSE POTS AN' PANS HAVE BEEN PASSED DOWN FROM ONE COURT CHEF TO ANOTHER OVER GENERATIONS! IF YOU RUIN 'EM...
I'LL STEW YA IN VINEGAR AND TOMATERS AND EAT YOU MYSELF!
I KNOW A CHALLENGE WHEN I HEAR ONE! YOU'RE ON!
Begin Operation: Beautify the Palace Kitchens!!
I'LL PROVE IT TO YOU...
BY SCRUBBING THE SCORCH MARKS AND GREASE OFF EVERY POT AND PAN IN THIS KITCHEN!
COULD SOMEONE BRING ME BAKING SODA, SALT, AND VINEGAR?
I'M BORROWING THE STOVETOP, TOO!
WHAT ARE YOU GOING TO DO?

はーん
SLAM
WHAT'RE YOU DOING IN MY KITCHEN?!
NOBODY TOUCHES THOSE POTS WITHOUT MY SAY-SO!
WHO DO YOU THINK YOU ARE, LITTLE GIRL?! EH?!
THIS IS SAINT SAKURA, CHEF!
SHE CAN DEFEAT THE UNCLEAN ASH WITHOUT EVEN USING CLEANING MAGIC!
I'LL BET MY WHISKERS SHE CAN MAKE THESE POTS AND PANS SPARKLE TOO!

RIIIGHT. THAT EXPLAINS THE BURNT BITS OF THE CHICKEN.
DO YOU HAVE ANY DISH DETERGENT? ANYTHING I CAN USE TO SCRUB THEM CLEAN?
WE DO HAVE HAND SOAP IF IT PLEASES YOU.
BUT IT WON'T TOUCH GREASE.
HE WASN'T KIDDING. THEY ONLY HAVE HAND SOAP!
BEFORE WE LOST OUR CLEANING MAGIC...
WE USED TO BE ABLE TO USE THE POWER OF SUGGES-TION TO CLEAN THE DISHES.
WHAT ELSE CAN I USE...?
HERE'S SOME SALT.
WAIT... WHAT'S THIS?!
BAKING SODA, MY LADY.
THAT'S SODIUM BICAR-BONATE, RIGHT?
OR IS THAT BAKING POW-DER...?
IF THIS IS BAKING POWDER, IT'LL FIZZ WHEN IT TOUCHES WATER...
AH, NEVER MIND. I CAN FIGURE IT OUT.
AH-HA! IT'S BAKING SODA!
NADA

CLASP
PLEASE WORK A MIRACLE...
ON OUR KITCHEN!
LADY SAINT!
PLEASE!
RIGHT THIS WAY, YOUR LADYSHIP!
CLUTTER
DID MY FOOD COME OUT OF ONE OF THOSE PANS...?
WE COULDN'T BEAR TO THROW AWAY OUR TRUSTY OLD POTS AND PANS.
SO WE HELD ON TO THEM, THINKING THAT SOMEDAY WE COULD REMOVE THE SCORCHING AND BURNED SPOTS ONCE THE CURSE WAS LIFTED...
BUT THEY JUST KEEP PILING UP!
EVER SINCE OUR CLEANING MAGIC WAS CURSED...
MANY OF US HAVE HAD DIFFICULTY CONTROLLING OTHER FORMS OF MAGIC, PARTICULARLY OF THE COMBUSTION VARIETY. HENCE THE SCORCHING.

OH, WHAT-EVER! NOW'S NOT THE TIME TO KNOCK HOLES IN HIS ARGU-MENT!
MAY I VISIT THE KITCHEN, YOUR MAJESTY?
I'LL AL-LOW IT.
SHWIP
THANK YOU FOR THE MEAL.
I WANT TO TAKE CARE OF MY DISHES TO REPAY YOUR HOSPITALITY, IF THAT'S ALL RIGHT.
MAYBE I CAN'T USE ANY FANCY MAGIC...
CINCH
BUT I HAVE TO HELP SOME-HOW!
LADY SAINT!
I...
I CAN NO LONGER BEAR IT, YOUR LADY-SHIP!

AS THE DEMON KING...
I AM ABLE TO LIVE IN THE LAP OF LUXURY BY THE GLORIOUS VIRTUE OF PASSIVE INCOME.
WHAT KIND OF REASON IS THAT?!
IS HIS ONLY OTHER OPTION WORLD CON-QUEST?

EXCUSE ME, LE-HAYE?
IF IT WEREN'T FOR THE UN-CLEAN ASH AND JUST, YOU KNOW, REGULAR DUST IN THE ROOMS...
HOW WOULD YOU TAKE CARE OF THAT? WITH MAGIC?
?
WE WOULD SWEEP IT UP WITH A BROOM, I SUPPOSE.
BUT WE GENERALLY EITHER THROW SOMETHING AWAY OR SIMPLY USE IT WHEN IT'S DIRTY.
BUT TO HIS MAJESTY ALONE, THE RULES DON'T APPLY.
IF AUGHT AROUND HIM IS SOILED IN THE SLIGHTEST, IT GETS REPLACED IN THE BLINK OF AN EYE. ♪
FOR REAL?!
WHAT A WASTE!
A WASTE OF MONEY!
WHY WOULD YOU EVER DO THAT?!
SIGH...
I'LL TELL YOU...
WHY.

CLASP
PLEASE WORK A MIRACLE...
ON OUR KITCHEN!
LADY SAINT!
PLEASE!
RIGHT THIS WAY, YOUR LADYSHIP!
CLUTTER
DID MY FOOD COME OUT OF ONE OF THOSE PANS...?
WE COULDN'T BEAR TO THROW AWAY OUR TRUSTY OLD POTS AND PANS.
SO WE HELD ON TO THEM, THINKING THAT SOMEDAY WE COULD REMOVE THE SCORCHING AND BURNED SPOTS ONCE THE CURSE WAS LIFTED...
BUT THEY JUST KEEP PILING UP!
EVER SINCE OUR CLEANING MAGIC WAS CURSED...
MANY OF US HAVE HAD DIFFICULTY CONTROL-LING OTHER FORMS OF MAGIC, PAR-TICULARLY OF THE COMBUSTION VARIETY. HENCE THE SCORCHING.

OH, WHAT-EVER! NOW'S NOT THE TIME TO KNOCK HOLES IN HIS ARGU-MENT!
MAY I VISIT THE KITCHEN, YOUR MAJESTY?
SHWIP
THANK YOU FOR THE MEAL.
I WANT TO TAKE CARE OF MY DISHES TO REPAY YOUR HOSPITALITY, IF THAT'S ALL RIGHT.
CINCH
MAYBE I CAN'T USE ANY FANCY MAGIC...
BUT I HAVE TO HELP SOME-HOW!
I'LL AL-LOW IT.
LADY SAINT!
I...
I CAN NO LONGER BEAR IT, YOUR LADY-SHIP!

EUUU-UGH...
LISTEN, I'M REALLY SORRY FOR MAKING A MESS.
BUT I COULD HAVE CLEANED IT UP IF YOU WERE GOING TO DO ALL THAT.
WERE IT NOT FOR THE WITCH'S CURSE...
WE COULD HAVE SUGGESTED IT CLEAN.
NO, I MEAN, YOU CAN CLEAN THINGS *WITHOUT* USING MAGIC.
IT'S WRITTEN RIGHT HERE IN *THE CLEANING AND LAUNDRY ENCYCLOPEDIA!*
NO, LADY SAINT! THAT WAS **YOUR** MIRACLE!
WITHOUT CLEANING MAGIC, WE HAVE NO CHOICE BUT TO WRITE EVERYTHING OFF.
IN ALL OF MY YEARS, I'VE NEVER *ONCE* CLEANED ANYTHING BY HAND.
THAT'S RIGHT! IT'S EASIER TO BURN ANYTHING UNCLEAN AND USE MAGIC TO REPLACE IT!
WAIT A MINUTE.
SO, BEFORE THE CURSE WAS EVER AN ISSUE...
THE CONCEPT OF CLEANING (BY HAND) JUST... DIDN'T EXIST?

WHEN OUR CLOTHES OR THE GROUND...
ARE MADE UNCLEAN BY FOOD OR DRINK...
OUR RULE IS TO REPLACE IT ALL WITHOUT A MOMENT'S DELAY.
YEEK!
WHOA!
WHOA, WHOA, WHOA!
SPIN
SPIN
SPIN
SPIN
WHAT THE HECK WAS *THAT?!*
HE REPLACED THE SOILED RUG USING DUPLICATION MAGIC.

LADY SAINT.
WOULD YOU PLEASE STAND?
HUH?
O... KAY?
YES, I SEE IT.
HUH?
UM...
I CAN DUPLICATE THIS.
HANG ON. WHAT'S HAPPENING?
YOUR PARDON, LADY SAINT.

H-HANG ON!
I-I KIND OF HAVE A HANDLE ON WHAT'S GOING ON HERE, BUT I NEED TO GET BACK TO--
ARE THEY EVEN GOING TO LET ME GO HOME BEFORE THE END OF SUMMER BREAK?!
I HAVE TO RETURN MY LIBRARY BOOK! NOT TO MENTION THE JUICE MONEY I BORROWED FROM MY FRIEND!
ガチャン
KRASH
SPLAT
SHOOT!
I-I'M SORRY...
CLEAN-UP.
ON IT.
RIGHT AWAY!

THIS IS ALL TO SAY, SAKURA...
THAT SINCE YOU COME FROM ANOTHER WORLD, YOU EXIST OUT-SIDE THE BOUNDS OF THE WITCH'S CURSE.
YOU ALONE CAN WASH AWAY THE UNCLEAN ASH AS THOUGH THERE IS NOTHING UNORDINARY ABOUT IT.
TO US, YOU ARE THE HOUSE-KEEPING SAINT WE HAVE PRAYED FOR.
WOULD YOU DO US THE HONOR OF STAYING IN HIS MAJESTY'S PALACE AND KEEPING HIS SEAT OF POWER FREE FROM IMPURITY?
ZZZ
ZZZ
(You need to learn)
(how to treat a lady!)
(Here's a training dummy! HAH!)
WHAT?
SAINT SAKURA, BEING FROM ANOTHER WORLD RENDERS YOU IMMUNE TO THE EFFECTS OF THE WITCH'S CURSE.
THAT IS WHY WE CALL YOU OUR SAINT. THE TOOLS YOU CARRIED WITH YOU ARE LIKE HOLY RELICS, AS FAR AS THE PEOPLE OF THIS WORLD ARE CONCERNED.

I GUESS THAT MEANS THIS WEIRD WORLD-HOPPING THING ISN'T A DREAM AFTER ALL...
THIS IS REAL, EVEN IF THAT WORD DOESN'T MAKE MUCH SENSE TO ME ANYMORE.
I'LL JUST HAVE TO LIVE WITH IT FROM NOW ON.
NOMF NOMF
FOR SOMEONE SO SUSPICIOUS OF US...
SHE EATS WITH NO RESERVATIONS.
THE *MISE EN PLACE* WAS HANDLED WITH MAGIC, NATURALLY...
BUT THE PALACE CHEF SAW TO THE ACTUAL COOKING AND SEASONING HIMSELF.
ほかほか
STEAM STEAM
MAY I CONTINUE? I WOULD NOT BE OFFENDED IF YOU KEPT EATING, OF COURSE.
MMF?
M'KAY.
MUNCH MUNCH MUNCH

DINNER IS SERVED, LADY SAINT. ROSEMARY CHICKEN IN A SOUR TOMATO SAUCE...
AND A SANDWICH OF SOFT BREAD IF IT PLEASES YOU.
IT ALL LOOKS AMAZ-ING!!
EVEN IF IT LOOKS A LITTLE BURNT.
THANK YOU! I CAN'T WAIT TO DIG IN!
MM! YUMMY! DIS IS BLISH!

WHAT?
OH! JUST...
IF YOU'RE THE DEMON KING, SHOULDN'T IT BE EASY FOR YOU TO, YOU KNOW...BREAK THE CURSE YOURSELF?
GRRGL
NOT EVEN HIS MAJESTY CAN UNDO A SPELL GOVERNED BY THE LAWS OF ANOTHER WORLD.
NAY!
GUURRRRGL
A GRUMBLING TUMMY IS A SIGN OF GOOD HEALTH, LADY SAINT.
OH MY GOD!
RUVAL SPEAKS THE TRUTH.
SAINT SAKURA IS HUNGRY AND IRRITABLE, LEHAYE. SEE TO IT.
FORGIVE ME FOR NOT NOTICING SOONER.
I WILL HAVE SOMETHING PREPARED FOR YOU AT ONCE, LADY SAINT.
YOU'LL FEEL BETTER AFTER YOU EAT.
SOME FOOD WOULD DO YOU GOOD!

HIS MAJESTY IS QUITE THE PUZZLE.
FOR A MAN WHO IS USUALLY INDIFFERENT...
HE CAN BE QUITE CHOOSY AT TIMES.
HMPH.
WOMEN WERE THE FURTHEST THING FROM MY MIND THEN.
AWAY WITH YOU. SHOO!
IS THIS DEMON KING SOME KIND OF A PLAYBOY?
I MEAN, HE'S HANDSOME ENOUGH TO GET AWAY WITH IT.
I CAN SEE HOW THE WITCH FELL SO HARD FOR HIM.
HE'S PRETTY MEAN, THOUGH.

I DON'T IDENTIFY AS A SAINT, THOUGH.
SURELY THE WITCH NEVER FANCIED HERSELF AS SUCH, EITHER.
SHE WOULD SOONER IDENTIFY AS AN INJURED MAIDEN, HORRIBLY CAST OFF BY HER PARAMOUR.
SPEAKING OF WHICH..
MAY I ASK WHAT YOU SAID TO HER...?
I SAID I WASN'T INTERESTED AND IGNORED HER. THAT'S ALL.
I SAID NOTHING CRUEL.
UH-HUH...
"Get on with it, Lehaye.
"I tire of this."
I CAN SEE HIM SHOOTING HER DOWN JUST LIKE THAT.
NOT THAT ANYONE SHOULD LOOK FOR FRIENDLINESS FROM HIS MAJESTY THE DEMON KING ANYWAY.

IF WE DO NOT APPREHEND THE WITCH AND HAVE HER UNDO THIS CURSE...
HIS MAJESTY'S KINGDOM WILL BE BURIED IN ASH.
WE'VE DISPATCHED SEARCH PARTIES, BUT SOMEHOW, WE HAVE FOUND NO TRACE OF HER. AND NOW...
SAINT SAKURA, THAT BRINGS US TO YOU.
THAT WAS THE ASH FROM MY DREAM!
EVER SINCE THE ASH BEGAN TO FALL, CLEANING MAGIC HAS BEEN RENDERED IMPOTENT THROUGHOUT OUR KINGDOM.
THE ASH FALLS AND CLUMPS TOGETHER, BUT WE ARE POWERLESS TO CLEAN IT.
WE CANNOT USE MAGIC DUE TO THE CURSE...
AND WE CANNOT CHIP AT IT USING BRUTE STRENGTH.
WHAT'S CLEANING MAGIC?
WHAT?
HAVEN'T YOU EVER HEARD OF IT?
IT'S A SORT OF SUGGESTION MAGIC!
IF YOU *SUGGEST* TO AN ITEM, "GET CLEAN!" THE FILTH IS REMOVED BY MAGIC.

SHE TOOK UP RESIDENCE HERE AT THE PALACE AND MADE HER AFFECTIONS FOR HIS MAJESTY *VERY* CLEAR...
BUT HIS MAJESTY WOULD HAVE NOTHING TO DO WITH HER.
IN THE END...
SHE CURSED HIS MAJESTY WITH A SPELL THAT WOULD MAKE HIS BEAUTY UNCLEAN...
AND FLED.
SHE CURSED HIM?
BLINK
BLINK
THAT SHE DID.
AND IN HER ABSENCE, A RAIN OF ASH HAS FALLEN THROUGHOUT HIS MAJESTY'S DOMAIN WITHOUT CEASE.
IT FALLS AS WHITE AS SNOW AS IT DRIFTS DOWN FROM THE SKY...
BUT TURNS SOOT BLACK AS SOON AS IT TOUCHES THE EARTH OR ANYTHING ELSE.

HIS MAJESTY IS, AS I'M SURE YOU'VE NOTICED, AN INTIMIDATINGLY HANDSOME MAN.
THE MOMENT THE WITCH LAID EYES ON HIM, SHE WAS SMITTEN.
SOUNDS LIKE SOMETHING STRAIGHT OUT OF A FAIRYTALE.

?
I FEEL LIKE YOU'RE LOW-KEY MOCKING ME.
LOW... WHAT?
IT'S NOTHING BUT THE TRUTH.
HMPH!
GET ON WITH IT, LEHAYE.
I TIRE OF THIS.
AHEM!
HERE ARE THE FACTS, THEN.
AROUND SIX MONTHS AGO, A PERSON FROM ANOTHER WORLD WANDERED INTO OUR REALM.
SHE WAS A TERRIBLY BEAUTIFUL WITCH.
WITH AN HOURGLASS FIGURE TO DIE FOR, AT THAT!

A FLY ON THE WALL, I SHALL BE~! ♪
THE FACTS ARE...
FIRST, TAKE A SEAT.
PUSH
HUH?
UH...
THANK YOU, UM...
SIR KNIGHT.
CALM YOURSELF AND TAKE DEEP BREATHS.
SADEEN.
LADY SAINT! WILL YOU NEED A MEMO PAD?
HERE YOU ARE, SAINT SAKURA!
ASK ANYTHING AS SOON AS IT COMES TO MIND, EVEN IF YOU ARE INTERRUPTING.
FOR YOU, PRINCESS MILIA, A CUSHION. THIS MAY TAKE A WHILE.
THEY'RE REALLY HAMMING THIS UP.
TAKE HIM UP ON IT, SAKURA.
LEHAYE CAN BE DREADFULLY LONG-WINDED.
FLUFF

STRUMMM
I AM CALLED...
RUVAL, MINSTREL EXTRAORDI-NAAAIRE!
I'VE IMPOSED MYSELF UPON THIS CASTLE, INDEEE-FINITELY!
FREE-LOADING AT THE MOMENT, BY THE WAY.
MURMUR
WHAT A WEIRDO.
ANY-WAY...
A MIN-STREL!
THERE'S A JOB YOU DON'T SEE EVERY DAY.
HANG ON... DID HE JUST SAY I'M "ANOTHER" PERSON FROM ANOTHER WORLD?
UM...
QUES-TION.
YOU SAID...
WITCH, RIGHT? WHAT WITCH?
AND SAINT? WHAT'S THAT ABOUT?
I WAS JUST ABOUT TO EX-PLAIN.
RUVAL, COULD YOU KINDLY CEASE FOR FIVE SECONDS?

I HEAR WE HAVE ANOTHER OTHER-WORLDLY GUEST AMONG US!
WHO IN THE...?!
AND WHAT'S MORE...
THAT THE UNCLEAN ASH IS NO MATCH FOR HER SCRUBBING CLOTH!
IS IT YOU WHOM THEY SPEAK OF, YOUNG MISS?
HOW ARE YOU CALLED?
POKE
ER, TAKATSUKI SAKURA...
THRUMMM
SAKURA... AH, SA-KURA!
YOUR NAME SINGS IN MY EARS~! ★
TO THINK THE *SAINT* WOULD ARRIVE ON THE *WITCH'S* HEELS! HOW TREMENDOUSLY *DRAAAAMATIC!*
WHY IS HE SINGING?!

MANY WOULD CALL CLEANING A FORM OF TORTURE.
WHY, THEN, DO YOU TAKE SUCH PLEASURE IN IT?
OH.
WELL, UH...
BE-CAUSE IT'S REFRESH-ING?
I GUESS...
SIGH...
LE-HAYE.
YES, MAJ-ESTY.
ALLOW ME TO EXPLAIN.
STOMP STOMP STOMP
BAM

GIRL.
COME HERE.
THERE IS SOMETHING YOU MUST KNOW.
SAINT SAKURA.
I'M TAKATSUKI SAKURA. JUST YOUR AVERAGE SEVENTEEN-YEAR-OLD STUDENT WITH A LIITTLE BIT OF A CLEANING OBSESSION.
I WAS MINDING MY OWN BUSINESS, JUST TIDYING UP THE SCHOOL OVER SUMMER BREAK, WHEN SOME WEIRD MIX-UP THREW ME INTO ANOTHER WORLD.
NOW I'M IN THE DEMON KING'S PALACE (I GUESS?), PEOPLE ARE CALLING ME A SAINT, AND...
HONESTLY? I'M JUST A LITTLE BIT OVER MY HEAD HERE.
HUH?

Chapter 2 ✦ The Saint in the Demon King's Palace

GIRL.
COME HERE.
THERE IS SOMETHING YOU MUST KNOW.
UH-OH...
WHA--
WHAT HAVE I GOTTEN MYSELF INTO?!
Chapter 1/End

SEE?
I TOLD YOU I WAS RIGHT.

SAINT?!
HANG ON. WHAT'S HAPPEN-ING?! WHY IS EVERYONE KNEELING TO ME?!
A-ALL I DID...
WAS CLEAN A WINDOWPANE...!
?
?

KNEEL
HOLY SAINT, YOU HAVE COME TO ANSWER OUR PRAYERS!
KNEEL
WHAT?

TREMBLE
TREMBLE
I CAN'T BELIEVE IT...
THE WINDOW FRAMES...
ALL THIS TIME, THEY WERE WHITE...
WHITE?! YOU FOOL!
HOW MANY TIMES HAS MASTER LEHAYE TOLD US HIS MAJESTY'S PALACE MUST BE DECORATED IN A PALETTE OF BLACK, GOLD, AND VIOLET?!
PANIC
WHY DID YOU ORDER WHITE FRAMES?!
F-FORGIVE ME! I THOUGHT THE COLOR WOULDN'T MATTER SINCE THE ASH WOULD COVER IT UP ANYWAY!
ARE YOU SURE YOU CAN'T LOAN ME A LADDER...?
IS THIS CLEAN-ING MAGIC FROM YOUR WORLD...?
MAGIC? WHAT ARE YOU TALKING ABOUT?
IT ISN'T MAGIC...?!
THEN... IT'S A MIRACLE!

ON SECOND THOUGHT, I AM NOT HOPPING ON SOME GUY'S BACK!
I MEAN, LOOK AT ME! I'M WEARING A SKIRT!
UM...
T-TELL YOU WHAT, SIR SA-DEEN.
I'LL GET THE LOWER SPOTS IF YOU GET EVERYTHING UP TOP. SOUND GOOD?
IF WE WORK TOGETHER, WE'LL FINISH IN NO TIME!
...
THE ASH WILL NOT BUDGE FOR US.
LIFT
GAAAH?!
SQUEAK
I-I-I'LL JUST WORK AS FAST AS I CAN!
SQUEAK
SQUEAK
GASP!
THEY'RE... WHITE!
WHAT IS?!
HE BETTER NOT BE TALKING ABOUT MY UNDIES...!

SHIIING
THIS PLACE HASN'T HAD A GOOD SCRUB IN SIX MONTHS, JUDGING BY THE WALLS.
NOT EVEN FIREBALLS OR LIGHTNING BOLTS COULD PENETRATE THE ASH...AND SHE WIPED IT CLEAN LIKE IT WAS NOTHING AT ALL!
DARN IT!
IF ONLY I WERE TALLER!
BOUNCE
BOUNCE
BOUNCE
HOW CAN THIS BE?!
SHE CLEANED THE WINDOWS WITHOUT EVEN BREAKING THEM...!
SORRY, CAN I BORROW YOUR LADDER?
WHOA...
RIDE ON MY SHOULDERS.
UH, THANKS...
ACK.
THE PIGGY-BACK POSITION.

IT'S COMPLETELY DIFFERENT FROM THE GIRL WHO CAME TO US SIX MONTHS AGO.
I DARESAY THIS WILL BE INTER-ESTING.
HEH!
WOULDN'T YOU SAY?
YOUR MAJESTY.
AW-RIGHT!
YAHOOOOO!
THIS IS HOW IT'S DONE!

ALL RIGHT! LET'S GET CLEAN- ING!
HMPH!
WHAT A STRANGE GIRL.
WITHOUT SPARING A GLANCE FOR HIS MAJESTY, RENOWNED FOR HIS BEAUTY...
OR EVEN ASKING FOR CLARIFICATION, SHE BEGGED PERMISSION TO CLEAN BEFORE ANYTHING ELSE BECAUSE THE ROOM REPULSED HER.

LOOK
UM.
MY BAG SHOULD HAVE BEEN LYING NEAR ME NEXT TO THE MAGIC CIRCLE. DID YOU SEE IT?
LOOK
SNAP!
THIS?
I BROUGHT IT ALONG. I THOUGHT IT MIGHT BE YOURS.
RUBBER GLOVES. CHOP-STICKS.
TRASH BAGS, DUST CLOTHS.
TOWELS, MASKS, AND MY BANDANA. THAT'S EVERY-THING!
DIG
DIG
OH, GOOD. EVEN MY LIBRARY BOOK IS STILL THERE.
CINCH

THIS PLACE IS DROWNING IN ASH!
I CAN'T PAY ATTENTION TO WHAT HE'S SAYING WHEN I'M SURROUNDED BY FILTH!
E--
EX-CUSE ME!
WHERE'S MY BAG?!
FWPP
REACH
AT EASE, SADEEN.
LET HER DO WHAT SHE WANTS.

QUIVER
ふる
QUIVER
ふる
BECAUSE I'M ABOUT TO SNAP.
OVER ...?
IT'S FILTHY!
AND I'M NOT GOING TO PUT UP WITH IT!!

THAT CASTLE IN THE FOREST OF MANAK WAS IN WORSE SHAPE...
BUT THIS PALACE COULD USE A GOOD CLEANING TOO!
AND WHAT WERE YOU DOING THERE ALONE?
I'VE TOLD YOU TO STAY AWAY FROM THERE.
I GOT LOST!
I TRIED TO GET OUT, BUT...
ASH OVER THERE.
UGH...
ASH OVER HERE.
CRUMBLE!
IT'S DISGUST-ING!
LISTEN, UM... LEHAYE? COULD WE PUT THIS CONVER-SATION ON HOLD?

THIS STRAPPING LAD IS SIR SADEEN, HIS MAJESTY'S PERSONAL GUARD.
HE CARRIED YOU HERE FROM THE FOREST OF MANAK.
NOD
UGH... HE'S REALLY HITTING ME WITH THE PLOT-POINT PUNCHES. THE GOOD NEWS IS, I THINK I'M FOLLOWING ALONG... FOR THE MOST PART.
AND THIS IS MILIA.
SHE IS THE PRINCESS OF THE FELINE DEMON BEASTS AND WAS THE FIRST ONE TO FIND YOU.
S-SO I HAVE THIS STONE-FACED GUY TO THANK FOR HAULING ME OUT OF THAT DUSTY CASTLE...
ふにゅ～
SMEOWSH~
I STEPPED ON A CAT!
OH!
YOU'RE ALL CLEAN NOW.
I AM!
AND I OWE YOU MY LIFE!
YOU'RE A PRIN-CESS?!

FINALLY, I AM PLEASED TO INTRODUCE HIS MAJESTY THE DEMON KING. LORD AND MASTER OF THE DEMON REALM.
DEMON KING... AS IN, THE LITERAL KING OF DEMONS?!
LIKE, THE GUY WHO SHOWS UP AS THE LAST BOSS IN VIDEO GAMES AND MANGA?

I AM LEHAYE, HIS MAJESTY'S CHAMBER-LAIN.
MAY I ASK YOUR NAME, YOUNG LADY?
HUH?
IT'S... SAKURA.
TAKA-TSUKI SAKURA.
"LEHAYE"... SO I'M NOT IN JAPAN?
MAY I ALSO INTRODUCE THE PALACE STAFF.
ATTEN-TION, PLEASE.
CLAP
SWOOP

FROM WHAT I GATHER, YOU MUST HAVE HOPPED WORLDS.
YOU WERE LYING NEAR A MAGIC CIRCLE CONNECTED TO A DISTANT LAND.
WOULD IT BE SAFE TO ASSUME THAT IS HOW YOU CAME HERE?
OTHER WORLDS? MAGIC CIRCLES? THAT DOESN'T MAKE ANY... OH! NOW I REMEMBER! THAT PATTERN ON THE FLOOR!
I WAS...
GRABBING A BOOK FROM THE LIBRARY WHEN THESE BLACK HANDS DRAGGED ME IN.
WHEN I WOKE UP, I WAS LYING ON TOP OF THAT, *UM*... MAGIC CIRCLE THINGY.
BUT OTHER THAN THAT...
OH, HOW RUDE OF ME.
SINCE WE CAN UNDERSTAND EACH OTHER NOW, ALLOW ME TO INTRODUCE MYSELF.

I'VE CAST A TRANSLATION SPELL ON YOU. NOTHING HARMFUL.
YOU UNDERSTAND THE WORDS COMING OUT OF MY MOUTH, DON'T YOU?
A... A SPELL?
NOW THAT HE MENTIONS IT...
PURR PURR PURR
YOU CAN UNDERSTAND ME NOW, RIGHT? OH, PLEASE SAY YOU CAN!
THE CAT SPEAKS JAPANESE!
KNEES WHAT? I'M JUST SPEAKING THE SAME OLD WORDS I ALWAYS DO.
THANKS TO HIS MAJESTY THE DEMON KING'S MAGIC, NOW WE CAN UNDERSTAND EACH OTHER.
HIS MAJESTY THE... WHAT?
PLOCK
THANK YOU, MILIA.
I WILL TAKE IT FROM HERE.
OH, THEY HAVE SLIPPERS!
SLIP SLIP

HELLO! DO YOU REMEM-BER ME?
BLAH
BLAH
BLAH
BLAH
YOU SAVED MY LIFE!
WHISPER
I SHOULDN'T EXPECT TO UNDER-STAND A FLYING CAT ANY-WAY, BUT HUMANS?
THAT'S A PANIC ATTACK WAITING TO HAPPEN!
THE CAT SPEAKS, BUT I CAN'T UNDER-STAND A WORD!
SIGH
SNAP
?!
HUH ?!
WHAT THE--?!
FWUFF
CALM DOWN.

ARE YOU FINISHED?
GET DOWN ALREADY.
I-I'M SO SORRY! I THOUGHT I WAS STILL DREAMING!
EEP!
GOING BY HIS FACE AND TONE, HE MUST BE TELLING ME TO GET OFF!
I THINK I PUSHED YOU DOWN IN MY SLEEP, SO, UM...
A-ANYWAY, SORRY ABOUT THAT!
I CAME TO SEE IF SHE WAS AWAKE.
THEN SHE LUNGED AT ME IN HER SLEEP.
I SEE.
CAN YOU UNDER-STAND ME?
HUH?
UH, SORRY! NO HABLA ISEKAI!

WELL, NOW. WHAT AN EXCITING TURN OF EVENTS.
I'M GLAD TO SEE YOUR ENERGY IS UP...
BUT I MUST INSIST YOU CHOOSE YOUR PARTNERS MORE WISELY.
?
?
HUH? WHAT DID HE SAY?
DO YOU HAVE EYES, MAN? SHE CAME ON TO ME.
IS THAT RIGHT? HM. I HADN'T THOUGHT SHE WOULD BE THE TYPE.
HRM...
I DON'T UNDERSTAND THEIR LANGUAGE...
BUT I FEEL LIKE I WOULDN'T LIKE WHAT THEY'RE SAYING ANYWAY!
...!
GIRL.

THE LAST THING I REMEMBER, I LAID DOWN FOR A POST-CHORE NAP...
SLAM
YOUR MAJESTY.
OOH!

HE'S GORGEOUS.
AND HIS EYELASHES ARE TO DIE FOR...
OH...!
W...
WOW. WOW.
WAIT! WHO ARE YOU?!
AND WHERE AM I?!
TROMP
TRAMP

I SAID NO!

IT'S FALLING SO QUICKLY. IT'LL REBURY HIM IN NO TIME!
HUFF
WHEEZE
WHY WON'T HE BRUSH IT OFF?
HE'S OBVIOUSLY STRUGGLING UNDER THE WEIGHT!

HUFF
WHEEZE
AGH...
WHO IS HE?
WHO CARES ABOUT THAT?! IS HE OKAY?!
STOP IT!
WHY ARE YOU ONLY FALLING ON THIS MAN?!
HUFF
WHEEZE

SHAAAA

ASH, FALLING LIKE SNOW.
CRUMBLING INTO DARK DUST THE MOMENT IT FALLS...
INTO PILES ON THE GROUND BELOW.
BUT WHY IS THERE A PILLAR OF IT HERE...?
WHAT A STRANGE DREAM THIS IS...

WHAT AM I SEEING NOW...?
OH... I KNOW.
THIS IS A DREAM...

OH GOOD... SHE'S ALIVE.
LITTLE SWEETIE.
THERE WE GO. ALL CLEAN.
AND NOW...
I GET TO TAKE...
A WELL...
WON ...
NAP...
FWUMP

I CAN'T LOOK AT A MESS LIKE THIS AND LEAVE IT ALO--
MYEWSH
ふにゅ
UH... HUH?
SMEOWSH
ふにゅ〜
I STEPPED ON A CAT?!
OH NOOO-OO!
AGH! WHAT A CAT-ASTROPHE!!
PAFF
PAFF
PAFF
PAFF
PAFF
PAFF
SPARKLE
HUH?!

AM I DREAMING?
OR MAYBE I'M DELIRIOUS FROM HEATSTROKE.
THIS PLACE LOOKS DESERTED...
HELLO? ANYBODY?!
I'M GOING TO START POKING AROUND, OKAYYY?!
BOOF
CINCH
MAYBE THIS IS A DREAM. MAYBE IT'S NOT.
THE WATER ISN'T SLIMY, AND I DON'T SEE ANY DISSOLVED ASH.
I CAN USE THIS TO WIPE EVERYTHING DOWN!
SLOSH
I DON'T EVEN KNOW WHERE I AM.
BUT LET'S GET CLEANING!
SWEEP
SWEEP
SWEEP

SKREE
SKREE
SKREE
WHAT ARE...
THOSE WEIRD LIZARDS FLYING AROUND IN THE SKY?

HUH?!
HANG ON, WHAT THE HECK ?!
FWIP
FWIP

WHAT WAS THAT ALL ABOUT ...?
...?
I CAN'T READ IT.
WHAT LANGUAGE IS THIS?
PAFF
PAFF
PAFF
FWOOOSH
IT'S SNOWING...? NO...

ぽ—ん
FLING
ぼふん
DWOF
OO-GH!
OWW...

WH--
WHAT THE HECK?!
WHAT'S WITH THE ARMS?!
N-NO! GET BACK!

GAH! MY BODY'S MOVING ON ITS OWN TO CLEAN IT UP!
JEEZ! SERI-OUSLY?
THIS IS CUTTING INTO MY READING TIME!
SHWOOP
HUH?
WHAT THE...?
HANG ON...
WHAT?!

AH...
THERE'S THAT DISTANCE AGAIN.
AH HA HA!
YEAH... I GET CARRIED AWAY LIKE THAT.
I'M THE GIRL WHO FORGETS HER WALLET AT HOME...
BUT ALWAYS REMEMBERS HER CLEANING ARSENAL.
EVEN I KNOW THAT'S STRANGE.
BUT I CAN'T HELP IT. I LOVE, LOVE, LOVE TO GET THINGS SQUEAKY CLEAN.
!
The Cleaning & Laundry Encyclopedia
Perfect Ed.
700 of our top cleaning solutions!
SQUEEEE!
THEY HAVE THE CLEANING AND LAUNDRY ENCYCLOPEDIA IN STOCK!! I CAN'T WAIT TO CHECK IT OUT!
HUH...?
IS THAT ASH?
FLUTTER
!!
BLACK STUFF?!
WHAT IS IT?!
PILED HIGH

ALL DONE!
GREAT WORK TODAY, EVERY-ONE!
YOU OKAY?
I LEFT MY WALLET AT HOME...
I'LL LOAN YOU SOME JUICE MONEY.
THANKS!
I'LL PAY YOU BACK THE NEXT TIME I SEE YOU!
YOU'RE STEADY AS A ROCK MOST DAYS...
BUT YOU CAN BE SO DENSE AT TIMES!
AREN'T YOU GOING HOME, SAKURA?
SEE YOU LATER!
NAH, I'M GOING TO HIT THE LIBRARY FIRST.
I WANT TO SEE IF THEY'VE GOT ANY NEW BOOKS IN.
ARE YOU LOOKING FOR NEW CLEANING GUIDES AGAIN? THAT'S SO YOU.
DID YOU KNOW THAT SAKURA MADE *ALL* OF THE CLEANING SOLUTIONS WE USED TODAY?
NO WAY! YOU CAN *DO* THAT?
THEY DON'T CALL HER THE SUPER CLEANER FOR NOTH-ING!
SHE GETS SPECIAL RECOG-NITION ALL THE TIME DUR-ING THE MORNING ASSEM-BLIES TOO!
WE COULDN'T MATCH HER IF WE TRIED.

I'LL BE YOUR SCRUBBING SQUADRON LEADER FOR TODAY. NOW, LET'S GET THIS SCHOOL SPIC AND SPAN!
MY NAME IS TAKATSUKI SAKURA. I'M SEVENTEEN YEARS OLD, AND I'M CURRENTLY IN MY SECOND YEAR OF HIGH SCHOOL.
LET'S DO IT!
I COULD REACH THAT SPOT IF I WERE JUST A LITTLE BIT TALLER...
WITH NOBODY ELSE HERE TO DO THE DAILY CLEANING OVER SUMMER BREAK, ALL OF THIS CAKED-ON GRIME WILL BE A NIGHTMARE TO CLEAN OFF.
BUT THAT'S WHAT MAKES IT FUN!

HOW DID I WIND UP IN A PLACE LIKE THIS? WHAT AM I SEEING?
AM I DREAMING? OR MAYBE I'M DELIRIOUS FROM HEAT-STROKE.
OOOKAY. LET'S TAKE A DEEP BREATH AND FIGURE THIS OUT.
I LIVE IN TWENTY-FIRST-CENTURY JAPAN. CHECK.
I WAS JUST HELPING THE BEAUTIFICATION COMMITTEE AT SCHOOL. DOUBLE-CHECK.
MIIIN
MIIN
MIIN
MIIN
LET'S SCRUB AWAY ALL OF THE MUCK AND GUCK THAT'S BUILT UP OVER SUMMER BREAK, GANG!

Chapter 1 ✦ I'll Finish Cleaning... in Another World?!

Contents

His Majesty the DEMON KING'S Housekeeper

Story by ✦Saiko Wadori
Art by ✦Mika Kajiyama

1

SEVEN SEAS

His Majesty the D

story by SAIKO WADORI

TRANSLATION
Nicole Frasik

LETTERING
Jennifer Skarupa

COVER DESIGN
H. Qi

PROOFREADER
Krista Grandy

SENIOR COPY EDITOR
Dawn Davis

SENIOR EDITOR
Shannon Fay

EDITOR
K. McDonald

PRODUCTION DESIGNER
Christina McKenzie

PRODUCTION MANAGER
Lissa Pattillo

PREPRESS TECHNICIAN
Jules Valera

PRINT MANAGER
Rhiannon Rasmussen-Silverstein

EDITOR-IN-CHIEF
Julie Davis

ASSOCIATE PUBLISHER
Adam Arnold

PUBLISHER
Jason DeAngelis

Maou Heika no Osoujigakari volume 1

Originally published in Japan in 2019 by Akita Publishing Co.,Ltd.
English translation rights arranged with Akita Publishing Co.,Ltd. through
TOHAN CORPORATION, Tokyo.

Seven Seas press and purchase enquiries can be sent to Marketing Manager Lianne Sentar at press@gomanga.com. Information regarding the distribution and purchase of digital editions is available from Digital Manager CK Russell at digital@gomanga.com.

ISBN: 978-1-63858-407-0
Printed in Canada
First Printing: September 2022
10 9 8 7 6 5 4 3 2 1

READING DIRECTIONS

This book reads from ***right to left***, Japanese style. If this is your first time reading manga, you start reading from the top right panel on each page and take it from there. If you get lost, just follow the numbered diagram here. It may seem backwards at first, but you'll get the hang of it! Have fun!!

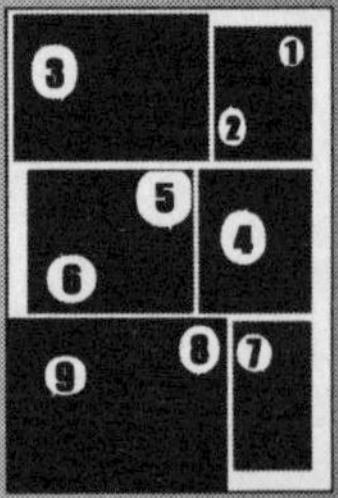